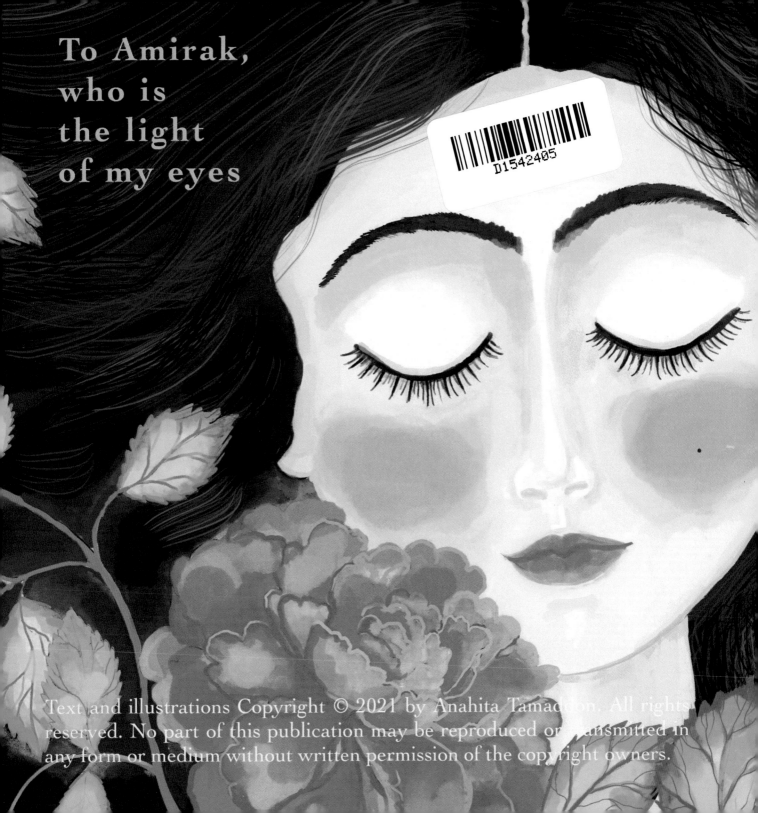

To Amirak,
who is
the light
of my eyes

در نوروز سبزه رشد می‌کند و قد می‌کشد.

Nowruz is Sabzeh (wheat sprouts) growing taller and greener every day.

Nowruz is the smell of blossoming trees.

در نوروز بوی شکوفه ها ما را بیدار میکند.

Nowruz is cleaning your house before spring arrives.

نوروز خانه تکانی قبل از بهار است.

Nowruz is clearing your mind and thinking good thoughts.

نوروز درباره پندار نیک است.

Nowruz is jumping over the fire on the night of Chahar Shanbe Suri.

نوروز زمان پریدن از روئ آتش در روز چهارشنبه سوری است.

Nowruz is your mom setting up the Haft Seen table.

نوروز زمانی است که مادر سفره هفت سین را میچیند.

Nowruz is about friendship.

نوروز زمان دوستی است.

نوروز بخشیلن و بخشایش است.

Nowruz is forgiving
and being forgiven.

Nowruz is creating and appreciating art.

نوروز آفرینش و ستایش هنر است.

Nowruz is remembering that every new day gives you a chance to start over.

نوروز آن است که هر روز بیاد بیاوریم میتوانیم از دوباره آغاز کنیم.

Nowruz is balloons flying in the air.

نوروز زمان پرواز بادکنکها و بادبادکهاست.

Nowruz is playing
music and dancing.
نوروز نواختن است
و پایکوبی است.

You can taste Nowruz in in the sweet pudding Sumanak in Tajikistan.

مزه نوروز در سومنک تاجیکستان است.

You can smell Nowruz in the aroma of
Sabzi Polo Mahi (Fish and Herb Rice) in Iran.

بوی نوروز در سبزی پلو ماهی نوروزی است.

You can touch Nowruz
picking fruits for
Haft Mewa (Seven Fruit)
dish in Afghanistan.

زمانی که هفت میوه را در
افغانستان میچینید
نوروز را لمس میکنید.

Nowruz is gathering around Haft Seen Table.

نوروز گرد هم امدن دور سفره هفت سین است.

Nowruz is helping others.

نوروز کمک به دیگران است.

Nowruz is being outdoors with
your family.

نوروز سپری کردن سیزده بدر در کنار خانواده است.

Nowruz is being adventurous.

نوروز مسافرت است.

Nowruz is giving and
receiving gifts.

نوروز دادن و گرفتن عیدی و
هدایا است.

نوروز به یاد آوردن نیاکان ماست.

Nowruz is
remembering
the great history
of our ancestors.

Nowruz is about
beauty and wisdom in
Persian culture.
Nowruz is about You
and Me. Happy
Nowruz!!!

نوروز زیبایی و خرد
فرهنگ پارسی زبانان است.
نوروز من و تو است،
نوروزت مبارک!

Nowruz is an ancient spring festival, which marks the beginning of the Persian New Year. Nowruz has been celebrated for over three thousand years and has survived many political and religious challenges over the centuries. Today about 300 million people of different religious and ethnic backgrounds celebrate Nowruz in the Middle East, Central and South Asia, the Black Sea and Caspian Sea regions, as well as Balkans and Caucasus. The worldwide Nowruz celebration takes place on the day of the astronomical Northward equinox, which usually occurs on March 21st. The celebration involves a variety of traditions and begins weeks before the actual day of the New Year. Nowruz traditions, such as display of Haft Seen, Chahar Shanbe Suri (The Fire Jumping Tradition), Tahvil (The Exact Moment of the New Year), Sizdeh Bedar (The Last Day of Nowruz) and many others symbolize and reinforce one's bond with nature. They promote values of peace and solidarity between generations and within families as well as reconciliation and neighborliness, thus contributing to cultural diversity and friendship among different communities. Untied Nations General Assembly proclaimed International Nowruz Day in its resolution of 2010, at the initiative of several countries that share this holiday - Afghanistan, Albania, Azerbaijan, India, Iran, Kazakhstan, Kirgizstan, Republic of North Macedonia, Tajikistan, Turkey, and Turkmenistan.

Countries that celebrate Nowruz as a National Holiday:

Afghanistan Albania Azerbaijan Georgia Kosovo Kyrgyzstan Iran

Iraq Kazakhstan Mongolia Tajikistan Turkmenistan Uzbekistan

Chahar Shanbe Suri

Chahar Shanbe Suri is the fire jumping tradition that takes place on the last Wednesday of the year. During the night of Chahar Shanbe Suri people light bonfires in the streets and jump over the flames singing: 'Zadrie man az to, sorkhie to az man' in Persian, which means, 'My my sickly pallor be yours and your red glow be mine.' The act of jumping over the fire symbolizes separation from all the bad things that happened in the past year.

Haft Seen

Haft Seen is a decorative table setting with seven items that begin with the Persian letter 'Seen'. Each item represents an important aspect of life as follows: wheat sprouts (rebirth), sweet pudding (affluence), dried oleaster (love), garlic (medicine), apple (beauty), sumac fruit (sunrise), and vinegar (patience).

Sabzeh

Sabzeh is part of Haft Seen decorative display of Nowruz. It is grown from wheat, barley, or lentil sprouts. Sabzeh symbolizes fertility of the land and rebirth of nature in the spring.

Sumanak/Samanoo

Sumanak/Samanoo is a sweet pudding made from wheat sprouts and sugar. It is one of the essential elements of Nowruz cuisine and is one of the centerpieces of Haft Seen.

Haft Mewa

Haft Mewa is a fruit salad consisting of seven items: green and dark raisins, dried apricots, almonds, dried fruits of the oleaster trees, pistachios, and walnuts. Families prepare Haft Mewa for Nowruz celebration in Afghanistan.

Manufactured by Amazon.ca
Bolton, ON

24782572R00017